NEW BOOKS FOR NEW READERS

Judy Cheatham
General Editor

Choices
Stories for
Adult New Readers

George Ella Lyon

THE UNIVERSITY PRESS OF KENTUCKY

This book is dedicated
to you
who made the choice
to learn to read

The New Books for New Readers project was made possible
through funding from the National Endowment for the Humanities,
the Kentucky Humanities Council, and *The Kentucky Post.*
The opinions and views expressed in this book are not necessarily
those of the Kentucky Humanities Council.

Published by The University Press of Kentucky
Scholarly publisher for the Commonwealth,
serving Bellarmine College, Berea College, Centre
College of Kentucky, Eastern Kentucky University,
The Filson Club, Georgetown College, Kentucky
Historical Society, Kentucky State University,
Morehead State University, Murray State University,
Northern Kentucky University, Transylvania University,
University of Kentucky, University of Louisville,
and Western Kentucky University.
Editorial and Sales Offices: Lexington, Kentucky 40506-0336

Library of Congress Cataloging-in-Publication Data
Lyon, George Ella, 1949-
    Choices: stories for adult new readers / George Ella Lyon.
       p.   cm.—(New books for new readers)
    ISBN 0-8131-0900-0
    1. Readers for new literates.
I. Title. II. Series.
PS3562.Y4454C47   1989
813'.5—dc20   89-38082

Contents

Foreword

The New Books for New Readers project was made possible through funding from the National Endowment for the Humanities, the Kentucky Humanities Council, and *The Kentucky Post*. The co-sponsorship and continuing assistance of the Kentucky Department for Libraries and Archives and the Kentucky Literacy Commission have been essential to our undertaking. We are also grateful for the advice and support provided to us by the University Press of Kentucky. All these agencies share our commitment to the important role that reading books should play in the lives of the people of our state, and their belief in this project has made it possible.

The Kentucky Humanities Council recognizes in the campaign for adult literacy a cause closely linked to our own mission, to make the rich heritage of the humanities accessible to all Kentuckians. Because the printed word is a vital source of this heritage, we believe that books focused on our state's history and culture and written for adults who are newly learning to read can help us to serve a group of Kentucky's citizens not always reached or served by our programs. We offer these books in the hope that they will be of value to adult new readers in their quest, through words, for an understanding of what it means to be human.

Ramona Lumpkin, Executive Director
Kentucky Humanities Council

Acknowledgments

My thanks to the following people: Ramona Lumpkin, director of the Kentucky Humanities Council, whose vision and hard work designed this project and got it funded; Judy Cheatham, project director, who coordinated and encouraged the work at all stages; Pauline Klein, office manager at the Kentucky Humanities Council, who handled the funds, set up meetings, and answered questions; Steve Lyon, my husband, and Jo Carson, a writer and friend, who read the manuscript and made suggestions; and the people I worked with in the Harlan County Literacy Program: Sister Mary Cullen, Mary Score, Alberta Abbot, Thelma Ball, Betty Colvin, Betty Eldridge, Judy Gingerich, Geneva Grubbs, Mac Hensley, Donald Honeycutt, Johnny Jones, Christine Kennedy, Lorine Lane, Phyllis Middleton, Peggy Owens, Diane Sargent, Diana Smith, Joanne Stewart, and Carol Warren. Special thanks to Atlena Ravizee and Rena Faye Fouts. Thanks to all for helping me with these stories and for sharing yours.

Dear Reader,

Here are thirteen stories, all about choices people made or didn't get to make.

All the stories are set in or near the same mountain community, and some of the characters are connected. This may be interesting only to me, but I thought I'd tell you about it.

Lena, the woman in "Crying," also tells "Getting Away from It All."

Joe, in "Working," and Herschel, in "Baptizing," are brothers.

Daryll, in "Making Something of Yourself," is Agnes's son. Agnes was the little girl in "Family Planning."

I don't agree with all the choices these people make. You probably won't either. My job is to let them tell their stories. If they make you mad or make you remember, I hope you'll write a story of your own. As the momma in "Singing" says, "Stories is where we come from."

For words,
George Ella Lyon

Getting Away from It All (Lena)

I'm going to tell you what happened at the supper table tonight. I had made meat loaf, and it turned out real good, firm but not packed tight. It had a red cast where I'd put in the catsup. I don't like a meat loaf gray or brown. It wasn't too greasy either. Jimmy is always after me to put in sausage. I'm not about to. His mother did, and it shows. I put corn flakes or bread crumbs or grits left over from breakfast. Jimmy and the baby gobble theirs down, but Lyndon just pushes his around in the bowl. I've learned not to give him very much, so there's always some left in the pot.

Anyway, I had made this meat loaf and real mashed potatoes. None of the box kind. As my mamaw used to say, "I killed and skinned them myself." With turnip greens and Jell-O salad, and corn bread to push it all around with, I thought I'd set a pretty good table. Not fancy but civilized.

You ever try to eat a civilized meal with three men? The baby's still in his high chair, but he's as male as the rest of them.

First thing was Lyndon didn't want to take off his cap. It's red and faded and says Stroh's beer on the front. Not that it makes any difference what it says. A cap is a cap. This one just happens to be ugly.

"We don't wear caps at the table, son," I told him. I could see cold water running down his dirty arm. I'd made him wash his hands. He leaned back in his chair and blew a big gray-pink bubble. It popped and made a skin over his nose. He peeled it off, balled it up, and stuck it under his plate. I asked the Lord for patience and tried to look just at his cap.

"Aw, Mom," Lyndon whined. "I got to wear the cap. My hair looks awful."

"It does not."

"It does too. I'm all out of mousse."

Mousse! I can't believe it. Twelve years old and he's got to have mousse.

"I'll get some at the store tomorrow," I told him. "Meanwhile, put your chair on the floor and take off that cap."

He glared at me. I looked to Jimmy for support. Jimmy—I swear this is the truth—Jimmy had his elbow up, hand over his shoulder, and was scratching his back with a fork.

Before I could stop myself, I said, "Lord have mercy, Jimmy, what are you doing?"

"It's that middle part," he said, his face all squinted. "I can't reach it."

Lyndon, his cap on the table at last, its bill in the bowl of greens, busted out laughing.

The baby laughed, too, and spit out his mouthful. Under the table the dog howled. Male, of course.

When he put down his fork, Jimmy like to broke my nose reaching for the corn bread. My glasses landed over by the telephone.

"I'm glad you all like your supper," I said. "I'm going for a walk."

So here I am at the Burger King. Turns out I only had enough cash for a cup of coffee. I'd forgot Lyndon took my five-dollar bill this morning. "Science fee," he said. Still, it's nice to sit here and watch the night come. Nobody belches. Nobody spits up. Nobody whose clothes I have to wash anyway. Women wash the world, you ever think about that? Get down on their knees and scrub its floors, its toes. All the time saying, "Take your cap off in the house, won't you honey? Remember which towel is yours. Don't throw food under your bed. If someone speaks, speak back. Don't just say 'Huh?' "

"Huh?" they say. "Huh? You talking to me?"

Working (Joe)

The other day there came this fellow, sent by the folks up at Lexington, I guess, to hang around the mine and ask questions. He was there when I got done with my shift. Puffy boy in fancy jeans. "Why did I choose mine work?" he asked. "How did I settle on mining as a career?"

If I hadn't been so dadblasted tired, I would have laughed. But if I'd had the strength to laugh, I'd have been mad, too.

"Where are you from, son?" I asked him.

"Down around Dayhoit."

"You mean you grew up in this county?" I asked. I couldn't believe it.

"Yes sir," he said.

"You grew up hearing and reading about miners?"

"Yes sir."

"Well, I reckon your brain ain't connected then." He looked kind of pitiful when I said this.

"Please?" he asked.

He had pretty manners even if he didn't have any sense. I looked at him hard.

"You're too old to be so clean," I said.

"Please?"

You ever seen a spring pup come out from under the house for the first time? It's looking for the world and looking for its mammy and not sure they ain't the same thing. This boy looked like that. I took pity on him, the lop-eared, clumsy thing.

"What's your name, son?"

"Willard Cox," he said.

"And your daddy?"

"Burl Cox. He was a preacher."

"Dead?" I asked.

"No," the boy told me. "He heard the Call in Michigan and took off."

"Too bad. Let me tell you something." I motioned him to sit on a rock wall by the parking lot. "If you had a daddy, you might not have such fool ideas about work."

"Please?" he said again.

"Careers, Willard, is what people have when they have money. They start out doing some little old thing and work their way up the ladder. The rest of us work at the same thing all of our lives. What we got is jobs."

"I see."

"No, you don't," I told him. "But I'm going to keep talking, and maybe you will. My daddy mined coal, first at Four Mile, then at Glenmary."

"And you wanted to follow after him?" Willard asked.

"No sir, I didn't. Going down the hole was the last thing I wanted to do. I knew I could get a job somewhere else, make a lot of money, if I could just get out of these mountains."

"So what happened?" Willard wanted to know. He seemed to be getting interested now.

"Well, for starters, I was no good in school. My folks kept me in, but I fought them the last two years. Graduated a dumbhead and proud of it. Not now. Then I went to Dayton to work construction with my cousin Mike. Our pay seemed like big money to us, but we couldn't hold on to it. Living cost a lot—plus we had to have a car, work clothes, money for girls and booze, and gas for the trips home.

"We came home a lot, and at first I didn't understand it. What were we coming back for? We'd got out, we'd got jobs, everything we wanted.

"Shows you how much we knew. The place you come from, Willard, is like a mirror. You have to come back now and then just to look at yourself. And if you've got people here, and you come back enough, you may decide this is the place for you after all.

"Mike and I kept working in Dayton, but we weren't getting anywhere. No promotions. Mike could hardly read, and I was too busy having fun to pay much attention to my job. Then things went bad. First Mike got hurt, then I got laid off. We held on for a while, but the truth was, we'd rather be miserable at home.

"What money we'd saved up North didn't last long. What work we could get here was digging coal. Then I met Rita and married and started raising kids. Mike got his fool self killed in a wreck on Black Mountain.

"That's my career, son, putting bread on the table. That's what I chose, to see that my kids had shoes."

Singing (Jeanie)

I'll be 40 in the spring. It's one of those can't-be-true things that's really going to happen. All I have to do is breathe through three more months. Most of the time I don't care. Shoot, I say, time is just a hallway to Heaven. Who cares about the numbers on the doors?

But there are other times when I look at my kids. Clyde is 14, Jessie is 11. I looked at them Sunday getting ready for the Martin Luther King march. I'm 40 years old, I thought. My momma scrubbed floors so I could get an education. I saw Watts burn, I saw King killed. And Malcolm X and Medgar Evers. I saw the Selma march and watched the 1968 convention on TV. I marched to get my hair cut, to eat in a restaurant, to try on clothes in the store. Do Clyde and Jessie have to do it all over again?

Marching is not the hardest part. Going to jail isn't even the hardest, not if you go together. Sometimes the hardest parts are the everyday things, the ones you do alone. They don't get on TV. Let me tell you about one of those.

I was 14, Clyde's age, when they closed the black school in Cardin and sent us all to the white school on the hill. Why didn't they come to our school?

"Not big enough," the papers said. "Not a suitable location." Not good enough for white kids, they meant. White kids don't do well with rats in the gym.

Anyway, we had to try to fit where we weren't wanted, where we didn't belong to anything. The ball teams took the boys in right away. They wanted to win. But what were girls supposed to do? I could survive without the pep club, the paper staff. The thing I really missed was the chorus. Cardin High didn't have one. It had a choir for boys and a singing club for girls, the Belle Notes. I told all this to Momma.

"Try out," she said.

"Oh, Momma, I can't do that. They meet in each other's houses."

"So? Ain't their houses good enough for you?"

"Momma—"

"I know what you're thinking." She looked up from the ironing board. "You're thinking they don't want you, and you're probably right. But they ain't heard you sing. Ain't nobody in Cardin, nobody I expect in this whole end of Kentucky, that can open just one mouth and sound like you."

It's no credit to me, but she was telling the truth.

My voice was a thing I just came with, like some fancy feature on a car. If I had brushed my hair and dollar bills had fallen out, I couldn't have been more surprised.

"Besides," Momma went on, "somebody's got to do it."

"Do what?"

"Be the first. Like your great-granddaddy."

"I know."

"Don't tell me what you know. You don't know anything about slavery time. None of us does. Nothing but what the old folks told us, and we got to keep that alive. Stories is where we come from. You pay attention. And you try out for that choir. You owe it to your people."

"I just wish . . ."

"What, Jeanie?"

"I don't know."

"You wish it wasn't so hard?"

"Yes."

"You and the rest of Creation." She was wiping sweat from her forehead with a handkerchief. It was one of those years when September was hotter than

August. "But in your voice you got something, Jeanie. God give you something you can *use*."

I signed up.

~

The tryouts were held in the music director's living room. There was a grand piano, a brand-new couch, 25 white Belle Notes, 12 white hopefuls, and me. Mr. Henley said they would choose 8 new members. We drew numbers to get the order in which we would sing. I was fifth.

The first two girls had voices that sounded like mice. The third was better, but she didn't have the nerve to breathe. The fourth girl, whose braces made spit catch around her mouth, sang "God Bless America" with plenty of feeling and no tune at all. Then it was my turn.

I started out quiet. I didn't shake the vases on the mantel till I got to "From the mountains/ to the prairies." I never did really let loose. They had all they needed and more than they deserved. When I finished, the girls just sat there. The one with braces started to clap, but her friends stared her down.

"Very good, Jean," Mr. Henley said. "I believe Brenda Wilcox is next."

Brenda Wilcox sang the song in neat jerks, as

if she were a music box. The next girl was good, though. Not a great voice but solid. And on it went. In the end there were two useful voices, two good voices, and me. That left them three choices for favorites, relatives, etc.

When it was done, everybody who tried out had to go to the family room while the Belle Notes voted. It took a long time. I kept looking at the red-plaid rug that was better than any coat my family owned. Then we were called back. We'd have refreshments, Mr. Henley said, while he counted the votes.

His wife brought out Cokes, cookies, and chip-and-dip. I took a few chips but could not swallow a bite. Strangest thing. I had to take what was in my mouth and hide it in a napkin, then put that on the paper plate and hope nobody saw. To keep from thinking about it, I tried to account for the smells in that house. No soap, no sweat, no cooking. What did these people do?

Then Mr. Henley came in with the results. Everybody listened.

The four girls I picked were chosen. Besides them, the Belle Notes took one of the mice, the music box, a girl who had no rhythm whatsoever, and the director's daughter. They did not take me.

"Sorry," everyone said. "Try again next year."

Well, from what I've said about my momma, you know I kept trying. The last year two other black girls tried, too. None of us made it. It was ten years before that choir had a single Black Note. You ever hear piano played only on the white notes? Not much music.

I used to think my activist days didn't start till I got to college. The end of the sixties and all that. But now when anybody asks what I did in the Movement, the first thing I tell them is, "I sang."

Family Planning (Agnes)

If you don't believe what I'm going to tell you, it won't surprise me a bit. My daddy and mommy were the best people ever was. He didn't drink, he didn't hit, he didn't run around. Every week he had work he brought home his pay. Every week Momma tried her best to stretch it, but it was useless, like trying to fit a crib sheet to a double bed. Not that she had crib sheets. Too many babies.

There were six of us younguns born fast and hard, not two years apart. I always thought my Momma was old. Lord, she wasn't but 30 when it happened. Nine years younger than I am now.

She was 30, my daddy 34, sunk in debt and younguns like quicksand. She was 30 and pregnant. Don't get on your high horse about birth control now. My people didn't have money. They didn't have a doctor. And you can bet there was no Home Valley Clinic where they could go for facts and equipment. You married and took what you got. My folks got too much.

I was nine at the time, nine then and nine years older than Momma now. I was nosy, too, and our house had real thin walls.

I was supposed to be asleep, but it was hot (right

around the Fourth of July) and too many of us in the bed. I could hear Momma trying to talk soft, but her voice kept climbing.

"What can I do, Jeb? What can we do? I can't have this baby."

"We'll make out."

"How? We're not making out now."

"Times will get better." His voice sounded weak.

"Not for us they won't. Not for people with seven younguns and mine work uncertain as rain."

"The Lord will provide."

"You don't believe that!" she hissed. "You just don't want to talk about it."

Silence, then the smack of his hand against her cheek. He'd hit her! I couldn't believe it. My heart pushed me to the door to go protect her. Then I remembered I wasn't supposed to hear.

A low moan came from their room. Too low. It was Daddy. And Momma was comforting him.

"Don't cry now," she said.

Next morning they didn't look any different, but I knew they were. It scared me to find out they didn't *know* what was going to happen, that Momma and Daddy were afraid.

That night I listened again. Nothing.

Next night the same.

But the third night I heard Momma's voice, solid as a fence post.

"I know what to do."

Daddy didn't answer.

"We'll send two of the younguns to my sister Nola."

"What?"

"She's always claimed she wanted some," Momma explained. "And Jack has steady work. Factory work is good in Cincinnati."

"You mean send them till the baby comes?" Daddy sounded as little as Willis asking that question. Willis is five.

"I mean till they're grown or we get hit by a miracle."

"Lexie!"

"I see no other way."

"But why two? You're not carrying double?"

"No. But I don't want to send one and have it lonely. And Nola's not easy. Whoever goes will need a hand to hold."

I couldn't see through the wallpaper and lathing and anyway it was dark, but I knew what Momma's face looked like: eyes hard, mouth stitched shut.

"You going to send Agnes?" My heart jumped. "She's mighty independent. She could manage."

"Not me!" I wanted to cry. "I don't like Aunt Nola! I hate Cincinnati!" I bit my hand to keep quiet, so scared I felt sick. And in the middle of that sickness and fear was a big hurt. Momma and Daddy didn't want me. They would give me away.

Then Momma said, "No. I'll need Agnes. She can help with the baby. I was thinking of Eva and Charles."

"Not Charles," Daddy said.

The hurt twisted in me like a washrag being wrung out.

"Willis then," she told him.

"Why?"

"It's got to be a boy and a girl."

"Why?"

Momma made a squealing sound and started to cry hard. I burrowed into my place in the bed. Eva was in the middle. I could smell her hair, a dense smell, like shoe polish. I tried not to think, not to hear, just to breathe forever, in and out, the smell of that coal-black hair.

Falling (Dexter)

The first time I laid eyes on Shirley Tackett, I said, "Whoa! I'm going to fall in love with that woman, and I don't even like the looks of her!" She was skimpy somehow, like the Lord hadn't had enough dust on hand when He made her. She wore lime green pants, too, and they were baggy in the seat.

What made me want to meet her then? The set of her shoulders, pure and simple. Here was a woman who had seen hard times and kept right on looking.

Sid Shepherd knew her, and he took me over to say hello. This was at the Kiwanis Pancake Day—I forgot to say that. Right smack on the courthouse lawn.

I said, "Pleased to meet you, Mrs. Tackett."

Shirley just said, "Should I know you?"

"No," I told her. "But I'd be proud if you did."

Why would a person who sees trouble coming just stand there and hold out his arms?

I do not know. I was widowed, lonely. I asked her to dinner the next week.

"Can't do it," she said. "I've got kids."

"Lunch, then," I suggested.

"Can't do it," she said. "I've got a job."

"Would you want to do it if you could?" I asked.

"I don't have time to think about that," was all she said.

It was two months before she'd go out with me, and then she had to be home at nine o'clock.

"Aren't your kids a little old to need Mama to put them to bed?" I teased.

"Old enough that I want to be sure they go to bed by themselves," was her answer.

Shirley had a smart answer for everything. Right before Thanksgiving when I asked her to marry me, she said, "Thanks, but I've already *got* a turkey."

She did marry me, though, almost a year to the day after we met in the pancake line. I sold my big old house and moved in with her. That was the only way she would have it.

"I'm not about to pull up my garden," she declared, "when it's finally put down roots."

I looked all over the 60 x 70 foot lot but couldn't see any sign of digging.

"The kids, Senior. I mean my kids."

I never liked how she called me Senior, either.

True, it wasn't just because of my age. I've been
Dexter Campbell, Sr., ever since my son was named
after me. But when Shirley called me Senior, it was
like she'd said Old Man. It was like every one of the
12 years between us doubled.

~

Our marriage started out okay. Shirley kept her
job at the discount store. I went on selling
insurance. I don't intend to retire till they lay me
out. And I thought we could drive to work together
in the mornings and ride home together at night.
Save on gas and have more time to talk. Not Shirley.
She said she needed her own car in town in case
anything happened to the kids. Also, if she had to
stop by Kroger on the way home, she didn't want to
do it with me.

"I'd rather take a two-year-old to the grocery," she
said, "than take a man."

"Why?" I wanted to know.

"I've lived long enough to know better than to
tell," she said.

You might wonder what happened to her first
husband, Roscoe Tackett. I've heard two stories.
One is he came home drunk one time too often and
Shirley got him ready for bed. Then she sent him out

the patio door instead of into the bedroom. It was February. He ended up in the hospital and lost three toes on one foot. Got divorced without ever coming back.

This is not how Shirley tells it. Shirley says they were at a party on Josh's Hill and Roscoe got so drunk he couldn't drive home. He wouldn't hear of Shirley driving, though, because the roads were slick. She had to get home to the kids, so she asked the people who gave the party to keep Roscoe overnight. He carried on when she left but then pretended to fall asleep. Later, still drunk, he sneaked out of the house and stumbled down the mountain. Next morning somebody found him in front of the post office. That's how he lost his toes and his happy home.

You'd think in a small town a person would know which of these things really happened. It doesn't work that way. Trying to sort out the truth from the rumors is like trying to count popcorn kernels as they pop. You might make it to six or eight, maybe even to ten, but then there's too many all at once.

As far as Roscoe goes, both of those stories could be true; he *was* kind of a boozer. I knew him from the VFW.

❧

What happened with me and Shirley wasn't like that at all. It started with sex.

Her idea of a love life was a once-a-week ritual, like going to church or cutting your toenails. Everything had to be the same, from the little glass of wine before to the hour in the bathtub after.

I thought this was odd, but I figured it would change when she got used to me. After all, she'd lived alone for several years. So had I, for that matter. It just didn't have the same effect on me.

After two years of marriage, I began to wonder. "Shirley," I started, one night when she got home from choir practice, "has it ever occurred to you that people make love on Wednesday?"

We were sitting at the kitchen table drinking reheated coffee. Shirley wastes nothing.

"Don't be disgusting," she said.

I had started out teasing, but her words made me mad.

"Or Thursday," I told her. "Or Tuesday, or even Sunday!"

"Senior," she said, stirring her coffee, "You are not funny."

"I don't mean to be funny." I took a sip. It tasted like wet cardboard.

"Well," she said, clanking her spoon against the saucer, "you can't expect me to take you seriously."

"Oh, yes, I do," I insisted. "But you never have. You've never taken me seriously since the day we met. No matter what I say, you've got some put-down. No matter what I suggest, you can't do it because of the kids."

"Leave my kids out of it," she said. "And keep your voice down. They'll hear."

I was furious.

"Let them hear! I don't care! This is my house, too. I won't tiptoe around like some visitor. I won't check your schedule every time I want to make a move."

"Some of your moves you can keep to yourself," she said.

She was eating by now, one of those heavy, sugar-coated pastries called bear claws. It made me sick.

"Why did you marry me?" I asked her. "You didn't want a husband. You wanted . . ."

Shirley stood up before I could finish. She wiped her sticky hands on a paper napkin.

"Now that you mention it, Senior, I do not know. I've been asking myself why I married you ever since the wedding. Maybe it was something in that

31

Kiwanis syrup. Maybe I thought it was better to be bored than lonely."

"What?" I stood up so fast I felt like I was falling.

"And it's not," she went on. "It's not better. You, Senior, are the dullest man God put on this earth. Here's your ring back." She slid it right off her scrawny finger. "I wish you better luck the third time around."

She held out the wide band that had been my mama's. I took it.

"I'll keep the engagement ring, though, if you don't mind." She admired it on her hand and smiled. "Something to remember you by."

What I did instead of kill her was grab the bear claws. There were five left in the package. I rubbed one all over her face, shoved another one down her dress, put two in the toaster and turned it on. The last one I put in the center of the table and drowned it in leftover coffee. Shirley just stood there, her stingy little mouth fallen open.

"There's a surprise for you," I said. "Have a sweet life."

Without even getting my coat, I went out the back door. Ugly, ugly, ugly Shirley Tackett. And poor Roscoe. It's a wonder he didn't lose more than his toes.

Marrying (Iona)

You're going to laugh at this. That's all right. I
quit worrying a long time ago about making a fool of
myself. The Lord did that for me, just like He does
for us all, from the get-go. So this story won't tell
you a thing that you don't know.

When Jake and I was courting, back in 19 and 26,
he'd come in from Virginia on the weekend. I looked
forward to it. Friday evenings we'd sit on the porch.
Saturdays we'd take a ride in his Ford and maybe go
to a picture show that night. Sunday meant church
and a big dinner before he headed over the mountain.
He was digging coal near Pound.

Anyway, Jake and I liked each other's company,
but I didn't love him. I enjoyed his stories and his
banjo picking. I didn't like his kisses, though. His
mouth made me think of wet socks.

Well, one night we was parked in front of my
Daddy's house, and Jake sort of mumbled something.
He had this habit of parting his moustache with his
thumb and forefinger over and over when he talked,
and his voice would sink down in his throat. I knew
he was asking something. I thought it was could he
take me to meet his mother at Thanksgiving.

Jake's mother was a strange-turned soul or I would have met her long before that.

I had barely said "Yes," when Jake grabbed and hugged on me and kissed me a big slobbery kiss. Then he said, "Come on, Iona honey, let's go tell your mommy."

I swear to you I did not know what had happened till we stood in this kitchen. He mumbled something to Mommy, and she said, "Speak up, Jake. I can't hear you for your toothbrush." Then he told her slowly, and I found out I had agreed to marry him.

Jake was so happy I couldn't tell him different. We was married 42 years when he died, and I never did tell him. Never liked his kisses either. But he was a good man, Jake was, clean–living and honest. I just wish he'd learned to speak up.

Making Something of Yourself
(Daryll)

I'll be 18 next month (the day before
Thanksgiving), and I've got to make some choices. It
looks like I will graduate in May. By some miracle,
my mom says. Then what? I can't go to college—it
would be like high school only worse. Besides,
there's no money, and I didn't do anything to win
financial aid. Not only were my grades LOW LOW
LOW, I can barely get a basketball through a hoop.
In Kentucky that's a crime.

But I never liked chasing things that bounce. Or
roll. Or fly up and hit you in the face. I've thought
it was dumb ever since my daddy gave me a little blue
football when I was three. "Wildcat," he'd say. "This
one's going to be a little wildcat."

Well, I wasn't, but he didn't stick around to find
out. For years I thought he ran off just because I
couldn't throw a football. Nobody told me any
different.

What I like to do is work at the Dixie Cafe. I
started in grade school, sweeping floors, taking out
the trash. My mom worked there till she saved
enough money to go to beauty school. "I left Dixie
grease behind," Mom says, "and took up hair oil."

Anyway, she liked working at Faye's better. Me, I can't stand the smell.

The Dixie smells wonderful: burgers, coffee, cigarette smoke, collard greens. You can order scrambled eggs from 5:00 a.m. till midnight, so there's a layer of breakfast smell, too.

But what I like best is the talk, which I hear while I bus tables and mop. Sometimes I wash dishes, too, if Missy doesn't make it. She has four kids, and one of them is always sick.

I come in right after school and work till 7:30. That's the latest Mom will let me stay on account of my homework. And chores. And, she says, "on account of I just want to look at you."

"Look at Peaches," I say. Peaches is my sister. "She's not as cute as me, but . . . "

"Oh, go on, Daryll," Mom says. "And don't get the bighead."

The thing is, Mom doesn't want me to stay on at the Dixie when I graduate. She says I should "make something" of myself. I tell her I *am* something. I'm a guy who likes to bus tables and listen to people talk. Mrs. Elam, who runs the Dixie, says I could work up to cashier if I came on full time in June. That would be more money. Mom could be proud of that.

But still she says, "I can't see what you like about that wilted old restaurant." *Wilted*, that's what she calls it. No hair spray, I guess. What I like is Mr. Welch and Mr. Dearborn coming in every evening to sit in their booth by the jukebox. I like one of them ordering the fish and the other asking for the special. I like Mrs. Grady and her daughter who only come on Tuesdays because that's Mr. Grady's bowling night. I like Angela Ann who stops in for coffee and cobbler on Wednesdays after she's met her Girl Scout Troop. Angela Ann's about a million years old and still goes by that little kid name. She groans when she talks. "Oh, oh, oh," she'll say. "I spent 45 minutes teaching my girls square knots, granny knots, and clove hitches, when the only thing they want to tie is the marriage knot."

Best of all is when the Fawcetts come, usually once a week. There's Freida and Ed (I don't call them that) and three kids. Whoever waits on them always makes the same joke when the kids get noisy: "Who turned these faucets on?" The kids are loud, but then they're kids. And they never throw their food. Earlbert mashes his peas and potatoes together. I did that once. Mom jumped up from the table and scraped my plate into the garbage. "That's disgusting!" she said. "Your father did that."

I stared at her. Most of the time Mom works at Faye's, takes care of us and the house as if Dad never happened. That part of her life is over, and there's no looking back. It's like changing classes at school. Bing! Bing! You march here, open this book, settle down, and then Bing! Bing! Bing! You have to go to another room and do something else. The math teacher could die after you leave her class, and they wouldn't let you turn back. Math was over anyway. Time for science.

It's never like that at the Dixie. Things kind of float. Old Mr. Kelly is eating cereal most afternoons when I come in. He was doing that when Mom worked here. He sits at the counter spooning All-Bran and frowning at the newspaper.

"Hi, son," he says, as I put on my apron. "Tell Agnes I said for her and Faye to keep them women beautiful. The rest of the world is going downhill fast."

Things do change at the Dixie but slow enough so you know what's happened. Like when Mrs. Lee died. She and her husband always came for chicken livers Friday night. Then she got sick, and he'd just stop by to tell us how she was. He couldn't stay to eat, so sometimes Mrs. Elam sent dinner home with him. "It's extra," she'd say. "Keep your money. I can't sell leftovers."

Then Mrs. Lee died. The Dixie closed a whole afternoon for her funeral. Now Mr. Lee comes alone. Not for chicken livers. He comes for spaghetti or pinto beans. And he has a little dog who sits in the booth with him. Mrs. Elam doesn't mind. The way I see it, the Dixie takes care of people. Better than some doctors.

Now if I can just convince Mom of that.

Cutting the Pie (Morris)

All my life I have heard how this is the Land of Opportunity. It don't matter, they say, what your background is. You can be poor, you can be black. By God, you can even be a woman. Hard work fixes everything.

Don't get me wrong. I'm not saying Americans aren't better off than some folks. I've just got questions. The other day I heard a kid, nice kid, privileged, say, "Sure I know the Golden Rule. It means the Gold rules. Right?"

Is that right? I want to talk about Equal Opportunity. I can't cover everything, so I am going to leave out the big stuff, like race and sex and education. Like where your house is if you have a house. I'm going to talk about teeth.

For starters, your teeth, like your bones and brain and all the rest, come from your parents. They come from your grandparents and on back down the family tree. If your mama didn't have enough milk when she was little, that shows up in your teeth. Same with your daddy. What I'm saying is, if your folks were hard up, you get short-changed before you're ever born.

Then if you are one of a string of children and

there is barely enough to go around, you don't get the
vitamins and such to grow good teeth. And to say
you don't go to the dentist twice a year is like saying
you don't go to the moon.

There you are, 13 and ashamed to smile. Sixteen
and putting a hand across your mouth when you
laugh. The only time you've been to a dentist is
when something had to be pulled. Your teeth are
kind of shadowy or crooked, maybe some of them are
gone, so you hang back meeting people. And they
judge you for this, *you* who didn't have a thing to do
with it.

So when you go out into the world and get your
piece of Opportunity Pie, just be sure you cut it up
real good. Not much flavor to it if you can't chew.

Pleasing (June)

I don't know when Bill quit talking.

I am not perfect. I will not pretend to you I am.
My figure is not the best, and I quit being young a
while back. Housework is not one of my interests.
Going to garage sales is. Others include baking
cakes, playing the guitar, and listening to sixties
music.

"You are such a child, June," Bill says when he
decides to speak to me. Usually this is when he's
caught me singing. "Next thing I know, you'll grow
your hair long and try to go back to high school."

Bill didn't know me back then, but he's seen
pictures. And I've told him about singing with The
Three Spirits. Me, my friend Amy, and my sort-of
boyfriend Russell. We practiced on Saturdays at each
other's houses and sang wherever anyone would let
us. Folk songs, mostly.

Russell and I wrote songs, too. I try to remember
the words to those sitting in the laundry room with
my beat-up guitar. Even when Bill's not home, I play
down there. I'm afraid his clothes or books will hear
me.

Some nights I say to him, "Can't we just talk?"

"What's the point?" Bill asks. "We've said it all before."

For some reason, last week that made me really mad. "Maybe we should split up then," I told him.

"Oh, sure," he said. "I'd get slapped in jail for deserting a child."

"The kids are 15 and 17," I reminded him. "And you wouldn't desert them. We'd work out custody." I couldn't believe I was saying those words.

"I'm not talking about Velma and Mark, you lump-head. I'm talking about *you*. You couldn't make it three days without me."

"Oh, no? And why not? I pay the bills, drive a car, cook the meals, raise the kids. What would I lose when you left?"

"A grown-up in the family," he said. "Someone to tell you what to do."

"I don't *need* anybody telling me what to do," I said.

"You don't? Who was going to feed the kids ice cream for dinner last week?"

"That was a celebration, Bill. I read about it in a magazine."

"If you read in a magazine to pour paint on their

cereal, would you do that, too?" He glared at me.

"It was to celebrate Velma passing math," I told him. "A whole meal of her favorite food. No fussing about calories or vegetables . . . "

"I swear you're making that girl just like you."

"Is that the worst thing that could happen?" I asked him.

He held the newspaper in front of his face. "Don't expect me to dignify that with an answer."

That is the last thing Bill has said to me except "I need socks" or "Where's my blue pants?" or "Take this to the bank right now."

My friend Yvonne says he probably has another woman, somebody young and skinny he met at work. Maybe so, but I do not see it. Bill wears his same old clothes and comes home at the regular time. As I told Yvonne, he's about as fetching as a paper bag.

She clapped her hands. "That's the best thing I've heard from you in years," she said. "Are you thinking about leaving?"

No, I am not. Not now, anyway. I am going to get a job. Bill will throw fits, I know. He won't yell. He'll just bring his grudge to the table.

He'll look at Mark and say, "If your mother was home long enough, she'd fry chicken till it's done."

44

Or he'll turn to Velma. "If you don't learn to cook, we'll all starve now that your mother's got this job."

Mark will just shrug his shoulders and go on eating. Velma will say, "Aw, Dad," and steal a look at me.

Even a year ago I wouldn't have thought it was worth it, getting a job, I mean. But now I see Bill's going to gripe no matter what I do. I might as well get out and learn something, earn some money. Maybe I could work at an antique store or a flea market. It would be like a garage sale every day! I don't know.

But I've got the newspaper here this morning, and I'm looking for jobs. Notice I don't say *Bill's* newspaper. Up until this minute, I've thought the newspaper was his. I've worried if the kids folded it wrong or got jam on it at the table. I've made sure the sections were in order. Just to try to please someone who couldn't be pleased.

I'm not like that, you know. That's the funny thing. I don't ask a lot, and I'm easy satisfied. All these years I've failed at pleasing Bill. I might as well try to please myself.

Trucking (Lige)

People are all the time saying that a dog is a man's best friend. I say a man's best friend is his truck. If he don't have a truck, well, I feel sorry for him.

The thing about a truck is you can haul almost anything in it and you still sit higher than the cars on the road. No offense, but I like to look down on people, see what they're eating, see if their hair's parted straight. And a truck ain't like a car. You don't have to keep it clean, just keep it running. Plus, there's always a little something you can work on. You can't work on a dog.

Sometimes I want to ride around in my truck, and sometimes I want to take it apart. It depends.

Riding around is for when I'm restless or when something's got me by the throat. Each gear I go through, I can feel something let go. When I see valleys down through the curves of Big Black Mountain, I start to breathe easier. A world that's got *that* in it can't be all bad.

Other times I'm not restless, I just need to think. That's when I raise the hood. So much in this life can't be fixed, that's why God gave us engines. I check the oil and water, change the carburetor filter (I use a piece of stocking and a rubber band). There's always belts to replace and hoses to tighten. A truck needs you. Now a dog needs you, too, but a dog *looks* at you. He needs you bad. That gets to a person after a while.

Sometimes I just start my truck up and listen. You can tell a lot by the way it sounds, like you can tell by a dog's whine if he's sick or only lonesome. Would you keep a dog you didn't know? People do that with engines all the time. I don't understand it. Then when something needs fixing, they hand their life to a guy in a zip-up suit. Not me. No buddy. If the thing's about to throw a rod, I want to know it. Besides, working on the truck is good for my mental health. While I got my head under the hood, whatever was on my mind just works itself out. When I'm done, we both run steady.

No sir, you can't ask for a better friend than a truck. It's hard working, faithful. Don't get fleas unless you let your dog sleep in it. Don't cause stray trucks to hang around. And if you do park it next to a bunch of trucks down at the store, it won't crawl in your closet and give you pups.

Crying (Lena)

I still remember the day I decided to quit crying.
We hadn't been married more than three years, and I
had cried a lot. Oh, I'd go for weeks, months maybe,
without a tear. I'd clean house only when Jimmy was
asleep or gone because it made him nervous. I'd
figure a way to keep us on our budget without letting
him know. I'd fix meals he liked and then just eat
yogurt. I was scared to death of fat. Should have
been scared of something else.

Anyway, we'd go along even as a tabletop until
something would upset the whole thing. It might be
an overload at work for me or Jimmy going for weeks
without looking for a job. All at once, I would blow
up, and Jimmy would stare like he'd never seen me
before. Then I would bust out crying, and he'd say,
"There, there. It's just one of your moods." He'd act
all manly so I could curl into his arms and soak his
T–shirt. Pretty soon we'd both feel better. It was
clear I was weak and he was strong and we were
balanced again like the tabletop.

Which I only scrubbed when he was gone or
asleep.

But there came a day when we'd worked our way
through the whole routine right to where I was

supposed to cry and something happened. All of a sudden I was a little girl again, and we were my mother and daddy. We looked different, and we said different things, but it all came out the same. Just like $5 + 5 = 10$, but so does $6 + 4$ and $7 + 3$.

I remembered how Mother would sweep and dust and shop and carry and cook and fold and scrub and never complain that it never ended, that we never noticed, much less said "Thanks." And then one day some little thing would happen—maybe Billy would drop his sock in the toilet and call her to get it out before he flushed—and she would absolutely blow up. "Why do you do me this way?" she'd say. "I can't go on."

When Daddy got there, they'd shut themselves in the kitchen, and we would hear her crying. It was like a tune above the low hum of his voice. Then he'd come out and take us in the living room while she went upstairs. "It's all right," he would tell us. "Your mother's just overtired. Be quiet for a while and stay out of her way." And that was it.

When I was little, I was so grateful to Daddy for making everything normal again, for being the calm one who never yelled at us. But that day, standing in my own living-room-bedroom–dining-room-study, watching it all as a grown–up, I saw what a trick it was. Daddy was saying that something was wrong with Mother, not with us who treated her like a servant. It was her problem. All we had to do was wait for her to get over it. Nothing had to change. Next day she would say she was sorry. Mother was weak and Daddy was strong and all was right with the world. How come I saw it that day when I had never seen it before? I do not know.

"This is one big trainload of shit," I said to Jimmy, right when he expected me to crawl into his arms. "Ride it out if you want to, but I'm getting off."

After a long time and a lot of fights, Jimmy did, too. It's not been easy. We've missed our old way of acting even though it hurt.

Of course, we still fight, but it's more interesting now. Sometimes it even brings us together.

The other day Jimmy said, "I've swept the whole house and taken out the cat litter, and you haven't dusted in a month."

"But I've done all the laundry," I said.

"Who took the baby to the doctor last week?" Jimmy asked.

I looked him right in the eye. "Who balanced the checkbook?"

"Okay." I could tell he was getting into it. "Who paid for the car repair?"

"So? Who took the car to the garage in the first place? Who dropped it off and walked to work in the rain?" I tried my best to look pitiful. Jimmy smiled.

"We did," he said, and I had to laugh.

I guess we can't keep score anymore. We're on the same team.

Baptizing (Herschel)

You been baptized? I been baptized three times.
My sins have been scrubbed on a board. They've
been bleached and hung out to dry. Jesus saves, but
He didn't save on me. I'm not sorry. I reckon I
needed it.

Here's how it happened.

I grew up on a little farm out at A-Jay, and we
went to Beefhide Baptist Mission. I was a big cut-up,
not really mean but not ready to say No to trouble.
When I was 14, I found my papaw's liquor jug in the
barn and drank till I like to lost my eyesight. That
was on a Friday night, and come Sunday I still felt
like somebody was mashing on my eyes with a hot
spoon.

Well, Mommy dragged me to church, and I
thought, "If I don't puke, I'll repent," so I did. In
two weeks I was baptized in Red Fox River.

Now I'm not saying that that baptism didn't help
me. It did, and I don't take it lightly. Lord only
knows what would have happened to me if I hadn't
had that little coat of grace.

The way I see it is I got cleansed there at Red Fox,
but the Holy Ghost wouldn't have much to do with

me. Partly because my heart wasn't right, partly because I smelled so bad. So I shook off the holy waters like some sorry dog and went right back to rolling in the dirt.

By the time I was 16, I had left the county and was hauling moonshine for an outfit over at Grundy. Now, they was smart. Gave me a big old Cadillac with a little bitty Jeep engine and put the liquor jugs right under the hood. My only fear was what if the car broke down. So they gave me enough cash for bus fare and said if the car give out I should hightail it to the nearest town and take the bus back to Virginia. That never happened, and I drove for them four years. Right down Big Black and into Cardin. Pulled in at a car dealer, blew the horn at the service garage. Up came the door, in went the load, and that was that.

I might still be doing it if I hadn't met Lorna Stanfill, who was working in a drugstore in Big Stone. I'd stop there coming back from Cardin and get chili dogs and Teaberry gum. After I'd done this a few times, Lorna and I got to talking. Now, she was older than me. Most everybody was in those days. She was pretty in the face and real—well, filled out. And she had this way of popping gum when she talked and lifting up ashtrays to wipe the counter while I ate, and, I don't know, I just loved her.

The thing is, Lorna was saved. Real saved. She lived with her daddy and his wife in a double-wide trailer in the middle of a sunflower field. And she had a three-year-old girl named Prayer.

O Lord. What could I do about that?

◦◦◦

Lorna always wore this necklace with a little gold cross topped by a diamond clip. The stone squinted when the cross moved in the V of her collarbone. The cross was framed by the V-neck of her uniform, too. That V made me think of another V just inside it. Oh, I tried to think about the cross, but it was so little and Lorna's breasts were so big.

I started carrying a red leather New Testament in my shirt pocket. She never noticed. Once I flipped it open and pretended to read during lunch.

"That's a good book?" Lorna asked.

"Best there is," I said, holding it up.

"I like the Old Testament better," she said, popping her gum. "Jesus don't scare you."

"Scares me plenty," I told her before I could stop myself.

"Why?"

It seemed I was too far in to turn back. She refilled my coffee.

54

"Well, look at it this way. After all them prophets, God sends us this baby with angels singing and everything to make us pay attention. People try to murder him, but he grows up. Goes around healing people and preaching love. Does not hurt a soul. He says we will kill him, and we do. You don't call that scary?"

"Not like sending plagues and burning down cities and turning folks into pillars of salt." She was trying to fit greasy menus back into a chrome rack.

"I see what you mean," I told her. I didn't really. I was took up short by what I'd said. It wasn't that I didn't believe in God. I was scared. Flat out scared of the whole deal. I put my little book back, embarrassed.

"You saved?" Lorna asked.

"Not exactly."

"Then come to church with me Sunday. Brother Smith can save anybody."

She was right about that. The way he preached I didn't even think of Lorna when we sang "The Way of the Cross Leads Home." I just went forward. Gave my heart to the Lord in the True Way Gospel Temple. Next week Brother Smith dunked me in the waters of the Nolichucky. I was really saved this time. Saved and fit for Lorna.

Of course, that meant I was unfit for my job. I couldn't expect the Holy Ghost to ride on a moonshine run, so I quit. Then I had to explain to Lorna why I didn't have work. I thought she'd kiss me, hug my neck at least. What she did was fold her arms.

"I'm glad you've got the Lord," she said. "He forgives such as that. Me, I don't ever want to see you again."

❧

Well, there I was: no job, my heart broke, and my ears dripping Nolichucky water. This time I wasn't scared of God. I was mad. I took a bus to I-81 and hitchhiked on to D.C. I've got a cousin who lives there. Ten days later I had a job on a mushroom farm.

It's not bad work if you like being cold and buried. I had time to think bending over all them trays. I thought about my bootlegging days, how free I had been driving the mountains. Now I was underground, under pavement, under buildings. Shoot, if I was going to work like that, I might as well go home and dig coal. I was half a mind to do it, but I didn't want to go home broke. I farmed mushrooms for three years.

All this time in D.C. I did not go to church. I

knew baptism only promised salvation, but I had
wanted Lorna, too. So I had a grudge. What good
was Heaven with no angels? I used to walk through
the city and look at church spires and see big old
fingers pointed at God. "Where were you when we
needed you?" the fingers asked. "Can't we have a
single thing we want?"

Then one Saturday I was out wandering, didn't
really know or care where, when there came a
November storm that would have shook the ark. I
didn't have even a paper to put over my head, so I
ducked into the nearest building. It was a church.
Dark with a spicy smell and candle burning. People
on their knees. "O Lord, it's the Catholics," I
thought. "I'd be better off back out in that squall."

I'd never been in a Catholic church, but I'd heard
about them: people kissing statues and waving
rosaries, and all the time praying to the Pope. There
was jokes about how Catholic toilets ran on holy
water. All this made me scared, but I was curious,
too. I knew I'd never go in the Holy Family Church
back home, and here I was in this big old Catholic
cavern, damp as the mushroom farm and a whole lot
darker. I decided to have a look.

There were statues all right. Women in nun suits
holding to crosses, men in Pope hats, candles burning
in front of them. The biggest statue was of Jesus's

mommy holding him in her arms. It was right pretty, but the strangest thing: Mary was barefooted, standing on the round world, and underneath that the old serpent was coiled and sticking out his head. It shocked me sure enough. A person ought to know not to go barefoot around snakes, I don't care who they are.

That rain had got me wetter than I thought, and I commenced to shiver. All of a sudden, I felt so tired I just wanted to sit down. It looked warmer at the front of the church, so I headed that way. There was no service going on, but Jesus was still lit up—a big statue of him nailed to the cross. They must have hung it from the ceiling on wires. He didn't have much clothes on, of course, and he was poor and skinny, same build as my brother Joe. In the churches I've been to you don't see much of Jesus, so I sat down to get a good look. Sat on the front row like I do at the picture show.

There was candles everywhere. You forget how different real fire is from light bulbs and radiators. I could feel the heat from the candles. I let my skin drink it up like I was sitting by the stove back home.

Up close I could see Jesus was lighter-boned than Joe. Broad enough in the shoulders, but he'd have to build up muscle to be any use on a farm. Then I

recollected he'd only done carpentry. That was okay.
It would come in handy really. Daddy always needed
the barn repaired or a new pen built for the hogs.
This feller would do, if we could get him down from
there. We'd find him some work clothes somewhere.
Mommy wouldn't mind. She'd take anybody in . . .

A hand touched my shoulder, and I like to jumped
out of my skin.

"Son?" It was a man's voice. "Do you need
help? You've been asleep here quite a while, and
we're about to start a service."

"Oh no, sir," I said, jumping up so fast he had to
step back. "I just came in to get out of the rain."

"It's still raining," he told me. "Won't you stay
for Mass?"

"Lord, no, sir. I mean, no, your father." I was
tongue-tied now. I'd seen he had on this black suit.
"I'm a Baptist."

"We are all God's children."

"I know that's the truth, but I reckon I better go."

I took off up the aisle before he could say more
and pushed the big door open to the rain.

The rain was silver, falling on streets shiny black
as coal.

"Come on, heaven water," I said. "I've been to the altar."

I was good and baptized by the time I got back to my room. Third time's the charm, though. On Monday I quit. On Tuesday I started hitching home.

Staying (Sarah)

Every day people gets married in the sight of God. They say "for better or for worse" and "till death do us part." Then they go out and do as they please. It is just the times.

On the creek where I live, there's not a soul besides me and Levi that's still married to who they started out with. Some ain't married at all. There's children all over, belongs to this one and that one. Step-daddies, single parents, boyfriends, we got it all. Sometimes I look down the road and wonder, "Is this people's houses or a motel?" I don't know who all the cars belongs to, much less the younguns.

It is not because the people are no good. People here is as good as anywhere else, some of them better. Besides, if it comes to that, folks don't much stay married anywhere in the country. Throw away the old, try something new, that's what the TV tells us. Marriage, dishwasher soap: it's all the same.

Not that I got a dishwasher. I've worked as a dishwasher, though. A dollar an hour when the minimum wage was $3.25. Around here you take what you can get. It ain't much.

That's a big part of the trouble with people's marriages. The way the law is, if a man has any kind of job, the family can't get on welfare. But if he up and leaves, they qualify. So you can see how if things gets bad, a man might take off. Stay gone just long enough for his wife to get signed up and then come back. Sneak into his own house. Go on working and try to make it look like he's living somewheres else. Then there's enough money to get by, enough to hold the family together.

Trouble is, it don't. Lying changes people. I've seen it happen many a time that what they pretended was true turned out true. Grown men hiding in their houses don't feel the way they did before. Neither do the women. Sometimes the man don't come home as much, or him or his wife take up with somebody else. And then things is worse for everybody.

If the man takes off, the woman is in a bad spot. She's got to have the welfare and whatever help public services will give her. She's probably not got a car or a job. And kids need clothes and school fees and medicine in the middle of the night. They need more, lots more, now that their daddy is gone. And she's got a lot less to give.

So what happens? She's liable to take up with somebody else. Might be a married somebody who can give her money along the way. Might just be somebody to talk to about the kids. In the end, it probably won't last, whatever it is.

But you can see how it gets started. When times is bad, people look to change their lives. Can't walk off and leave a boss that treats you like dirt, but you can sure slam the door on your wife and kids. Can't find any pleasure in a life tied to three babies, but you can sure take a ride with that man from over the hill. If you can't change what needs changing, well sir, you'll change something else. Chances are it'll be the very thing that should have stayed the same.

Levi and me, we've been together all our lives. We set eyes on each other, went to courting, and that was that. I'm not saying we haven't had our fights. Lord knows, Levi's stubborn. Probably knows I am, too. But we've held together, raised four younguns. Got through times that seemed like all work and no love. But we stuck together. Would you cut off your arm just because it pained you? No, you'd do what you could to get it to heal. "For better or for worse," we said, and I reckon we meant it. Forty years have come and gone, and we're still right here.

About the Author

A native of Harlan, Kentucky, George Ella Lyon attended Centre College, the University of Arkansas, and Indiana University. Her works include *Mountain*, poems; *Braids*, a play; *Borrowed Children* and *Red Rover, Red Rover*, novels; and four picture books, *Together*, *A B Cedar*, *A Regular Rolling Noah*, and *Father Time and the Day Boxes*. Lyon works as a freelance writer and teacher in Lexington, Kentucky. She and her husband, musician Steven Lyon, have two sons.